"Time to tidy up!" Amber's mum called from the top of the basement steps.

"Oh Mum, can't we do it later?" Amber called back.

"*Much* later!" Pearl giggled.

"Cool!" Lily liked tidying. "Hey, Amber, pass me that witch's hat. Don't tread on it. You'll make it wonky." Picking some crushed fairy wings off the floor as she

5

talked, Lily placed the dressing-up clothes in the box.

"Stop!" Amber cried. "Just looking at you makes me feel dizzy!"

Lily tutted and picked up a silver skirt. She swished it into the box.

"Hey, I wanted to try that on!" Pearl protested as Lily whisked a big hat with purple feathers out of her hands.

"Grumble-grumble," Lily muttered. She dumped a blue velvet jacket on top of the frilly skirt. "This room is looking so much better already!"

Frowning, Pearl turned to Amber. "Are you thinking what I'm thinking?"

Amber stared at Lily's busy back view. Lily was bending over the dressing-up box, sorting out the boots and shoes into

6

one corner, skirts into another.

"Hats to the right, shawls to the left," Lily mumbled.

"I *am* thinking what you're thinking," Amber told Pearl.

"Shirts and blouses in the middle . . ."

"Ready?" Pearl hissed.

"Go!" Amber nodded. She and Pearl dashed towards Lily and tipped her forward.

"Whoa!" Lily cried. "Hey, stop that! Wait! Whoa, I'm falling . . . Help!"

Straight into the jumble of clothes, down amongst the hats and scarves, the Spiderman mask, the fairy wand.

"Ha!" Amber and Pearl cried.

"Let me out!" Lily cried as the lid of the box accidentally slammed shut.

"*Let me out!*" Pearl and Amber heard the muffled shout. They ran to help but it was too late.

Inside the box, Lily sank through the soft silks and shiny satins. The dressing-up clothes seemed to glow with soft red and blue lights which grew brighter and soon turned to dazzling white.

"Help!" Lily cried as she sank deeper and the light dazzled her and made her dizzy. It sparkled like ice on window panes, like diamonds, like snow . . .

8

"Oops!" Pearl saw a thin shaft of light shine out from under the rim of Amber's dressing-up box. "It can't be . . .!"

"Yes, it can!" Amber ran to lift the lid. The light blinded her and she staggered back. "It's happening again. Lily has been whooshed away!"

Tramp-tramp-tramp! Through the snow the seven dwarves marched. Behind them the Prince of Ice Mountain rode on his chestnut horse.

The forest trees hung low over the track. Black crows flapped their wings and rose into the morning air.

"Keep up, Hans!" Tom called from the front. "Walt, don't stray from the path. Roly, let me know if you need to rest."

"No, we must carry on until we reach the shelter," stout Roly gasped. "There is no time to lose."

Tramp-tramp-tramp!

Lily whooshed through the snow-filled air. Wrapped in a crimson cloak, she soared through clouds which carried a million snowflakes.

Floating on a snowstorm, gently lowered through the dark trees, she came

10

to rest at the entrance to the secret shelter where the dwarves had left her.

She lay on the ground and snowflakes landed on her cold cheeks. Her eyes were closed. She did not seem to breathe.

For once the dwarves didn't sing as they marched. There was fear in the air – in the croak of the black crows and the eerie silence of their own footfall.

"How soon do we reach the shelter?" the

Prince of Ice Mountain asked.

He had been ordered by his mother, the Queen of Ice Mountain, to save the girl from wicked Queen Serena.

"Snow White is lovely as the day," the Queen had told him. "Her hair is black as jet, her cheeks as white as snow."

"Very soon," Jack promised the Prince. But his heart was squeezed tight by fear of what they might find.

"Beyond this ridge." Pete recognised the rocks. He strode impatiently ahead.

It was clumsy Hans who veered off from the path and took a short cut towards the entrance to the old mine which they had chosen as their secret shelter. "Snow White, we're back!" he called. "We have brought the Prince of Ice

Mountain with us, to rescue you!"

"Snow White, where are you?" Walt called, not noticing the snow-covered shape lying by the entrance. He opened the creaking wooden door and peered inside.

Pete, Jack, Roly, Will and Tom joined in the search. The Prince dismounted from his horse.

"She's not here!" Will and Jack searched with Walt inside the old mine.

Pete, Roly and Tom stopped Hans from blundering on through the forest. "Stop, brother," they told him. "If Snow White has wandered away from the shelter we have no hope of finding her until the snowstorm lifts."

Hans hung his head and sighed.

But then the Prince of Ice Mountain saw

the shape on the ground. He knelt and brushed the snow away, seeing that the girl's hair was black as jet, as his mother described. "Over here!" he called softly.

The seven brothers gathered round. They bent over the figure of Snow White.

"We are too late!" Tom said in a broken voice.

A snowflake melted on Lily's eyelash and ran down her cheek like a single tear.

14

2

"Her face is lovely," the Prince said, bending forward. He brushed more snow from Lily's frozen cheek and gently raised her head.

"Too late!" Hans and Walt murmured again. The dwarves clasped their hands and bowed their heads.

As the Prince raised Lily from the snow-drift, her hood fell back and loosened the

15

comb which wicked Queenie had forced into her hair.

"Carry her indoors," Jack told the Prince sorrowfully.

Pete held open the door to the shelter. Tom cleared a space on the low, rough table.

The young Prince of Ice Mountain laid Lily down. He stroked her glossy hair and the poisoned comb fell to the ground.

Lily took a breath. Her eyelids fluttered.

"She is alive!" the Prince whispered.

Roly rushed to light a fire. Tom wrapped Lily in a warm blanket. Pete and Will lit candles. Hans and Jack sat by Lily and held her hand.

Seeing the Queen's comb on the floor,

Walt stamped on it and
ground it into the dirt.

After a while Lily
opened her eyes.
She looked up
at the handsome
face of the Prince
of Ice Mountain.

At first his features were blurred. Then
she saw that his eyes were blue as a
mountain lake. He wore a hat of deep
blue velvet with a white feather. His coat
was blue to match.

"What happened? Where am I?" Lily
wondered aloud.

"You are safe," the Prince said. "These
seven brave brothers climbed Ice
Mountain to ask for our help. My mother,

the Queen, will gladly give you shelter."

"That's good," Lily whispered. She took a deep breath, gazing round the candlelit shelter at seven relieved faces.

"Snow White, you must ride on my horse," the Prince decided. "The brothers will pack their belongings and follow us on foot."

"A good plan," Pete agreed. "We won't be far behind."

"Yes, yes." Jack backed him up. "The sooner you reach the good Queen's palace the better, my dear."

"But you won't be long?" Lily was feeling stronger. She sat up straight, embarrassed to see that the Prince was still gazing at her adoringly. *Less of the lovey-dovey looks!* she thought with a grimace.

18

"We'll be quick," Will promised, stuffing his spare clothes into a coarse sack hanging behind the door.

"Swift as an arrow," Roly told her. "We'll be there for supper – meat pie and a mountain of mashed potatoes, if I have my way!"

Smiling, Lily stood up and wrapped her

cloak around her. She raised her hood. "OK, I'm ready," she told the Prince.

Once more Pete held the door open. "Look after her, upon your life!" he muttered.

The Prince bowed then nodded. He lifted Lily on to Phoebe, his chestnut mare. Then he led them back the way he had come.

"Aaah-choo!" Prince Lovelace was out in the storm, stumbling through the forest, blinded by the snow.

"Upon my life, I am so c-c-cold!" he complained. "I swear I will freeze to death if I stay out much longer. Aah-choo!"

His horse sank up to its belly in frozen drifts. The Prince leaned into the wind, grumbling and sneezing as he made his way towards Ice Mountain.

"How far now?" Lily asked, staring straight ahead between the horse's ears.

"Uh – um – oh, not far," the Prince replied. He was still wearing the soppy expression, concentrating on Lily instead of looking where he was going.

Lily sighed. It was one thing reading a fairy story about a handsome prince falling in love with a princess, quite another when it happened for real. *I wish he'd stop staring!* she thought.

"You see the white mountain ahead?" the Prince asked. "There is a palace on a ledge overlooking the valley. Its windows glint in the sun."

21

Lily squinted then nodded.

"That is our journey's end."

"Cool. I mean, good. At least the snow has stopped." Lily was happy to chat about the boring weather.

"And now the sun is shining," the Prince noted with a happy sigh.

As they came out of the forest and

began to climb Ice Mountain, Lily glanced over her shoulder. *Get a move on Tom, Jack and Will! Help me out, Pete and Roly.* The journey seemed endless. Phoebe had slowed to a steady plod and still the shining palace seemed a long way off.

Walt and Hans, where are you when I need you? The Prince is still giving me the gooey looks and I can't think of a single thing to say!

"Drat this snow!" Wrapped in a black cloak and hat, Prince Lovelace coughed and spluttered as he reached the edge of the forest. "And drat Her Most Royal Highness for turning against me and throwing me out into the forest to be eaten by wolves! Aah-choo!"

23

Phoebe heard a distant sneeze and stopped in her tracks.

"Walk on." The Prince of Ice Mountain tugged firmly at the reins.

But the horse pricked her ears to listen again.

"I have served Her Most Royal Highness loyally," Prince Lovelace complained bitterly as his horse stumbled on. He noticed that the snow had finally stopped but that the wind still blew strongly. "And now I am punished for my pains," he muttered. "Forced to wander like a stranger in my own land!"

Neeeighhhh! Phoebe pranced and called loudly.

From between two high rocks a grey horse and a dark rider came into view.

The Prince of Ice Mountain and Lily stared at him through narrowed eyes.

"Aah-choo! How miserable I am!"

Lily heard the high, weedy voice and gasped. *Prince Lovelace!*

The Prince of Ice Mountain put his hand to his sword, ready to defend Lily.

"Most miserable and c-c-cold!" the weedy Prince sniffed. Then he looked up and saw that his way was blocked. He stared hard at Lily's dark hair and pale face. "G-g-good heavens!" he cried.

Lily tried to hide behind her hood, but it was no good.

"I can scarce believe it. Is it really you?" Prince Lovelace asked. "Yes – it *is* Snow White, here – before my very eyes!"

3

Lily recognised Prince Pester-Face and groaned.

Here was the nerd who had been all over her like a rash on her first trip to Snow-White world. "Please dance with me, please sit next to me!" – until she was sick of him.

Then suddenly he'd switched sides and started spying for Queenie. "Your Most

Royal Highness, I am your loyal servant. Your wish is my command!"

Lily leaned sideways in her saddle. "Don't trust him!" she warned the Prince of Ice Mountain.

The handsome Prince stood his ground as Pester-Face pranced towards them. "Stop, sir, and tell us your business!" he demanded.

"I am Prince Lovelace. Pray, sir, who are you?"

Lily's Prince was too proud to answer. "Why are you riding through the forest in a snowstorm when any wise man would rest by his fireside?" he asked sternly.

Pester-Face drew himself up tall. "I will not answer your rude questions, for I am a royal Prince. And I challenge you, sir – tell me why you are creeping through the forest like a thief with Snow White when the whole world is searching for her?"

Uh-oh, we're in trouble! Lily thought.

"We are not creeping, as you put it. Snow White rides with me to my mother's palace on Ice Mountain," the Prince replied haughtily.

Definitely in trouble! Lily groaned. She knew for sure that nerdy Pester-Face would gallop back to tell Queenie she was still alive.

But she was wrong. "I will ride with you," he said quickly, seeing his own road to safety. "And you, sir, will step back and let me lead the lovely Snow White. From now on I will look after her!"

"Erm, hang on a second!" Lily protested

as Pester-Face seized Phoebe's reins.

The Prince of Ice Mountain drew his sword against his rival. "Never!" he declared. "I have sworn to protect Snow White with my life. Turn around and fight, you scoundrel!"

So Lovelace slid clumsily from his horse and drew his own sword.

"Stop!" Lily cried. *Double trouble! Disaster. Help!*

As Prince Lovelace clashed swords with the Prince of Ice Mountain, his skinny legs began to shake. His sword felt heavy and he stumbled.

Clash-clash! The metal blades rang out. Lovelace staggered back against a tree. The Prince of Ice Mountain raised his sword above his head.

"Don't!" Lily pleaded. She definitely didn't want anyone getting injured on her account.

The handsome Prince stayed his sword. It gave Pester-Face time to launch himself forward and head-butt his rival in the belly.

"Oof!" The Prince of Ice Mountain bent double and it was Pester-Face's turn to raise his sword.

30

"Oh no you don't!' Leaping from the saddle, Lily piggy-backed Pester-Face. She clung like a monkey and forced him to drop his sword. "Say you give in!" she demanded. "Go on – give in!"

"I g-g-ive in!" Lovelace stammered and the Prince of Ice Mountain lowered his sword.

Satisfied, Lily jumped down and smoothed her red satin skirt.

"Can he come with us if he promises to behave?" Lily asked. After all, she didn't want Pester-Face to freeze to death or be eaten by wolves out here. "I'm guessing he's run away from Queenie and needs somewhere to stay."

Still trembling, Prince Lovelace remounted his own horse. "Aahchoo!"

The Prince of Ice Mountain considered Lily's unusual request. "I must find out more about the man before we give him shelter," he decided, turning back to Lovelace.

But quick-thinking Pester-Face had already made a new plan. *I will ride back to the palace,* he told himself. "Aahchoo!" *I have news of Snow White which Queen Serena will want to hear!*

So he didn't hang around to face the Prince's questions. Instead, he tugged on the reins and wheeled his horse around, giving him a hard kick and sending him galloping off through the snow.

"Who was the rider we saw just now?" Jack was the first of the brothers to arrive upon the scene.

The seven dwarves had packed their belongings and hurried after Snow White and the Prince of Ice Mountain. They'd marched quickly out of the forest, singing their mining song. Now they'd come across the scene of the recent sword fight.

"Don't ask," Lily groaned. How stupid was she, even to think of trying to help Pester-Face?

"He was a scoundrel," the Prince of Ice Mountain told Jack abruptly. "And now we must hurry to my mother's palace and to safety."

*

The palace on Ice Mountain looked out over a range of snowy peaks. It perched in a white wilderness, its round towers soaring upwards into a cloudless sky.

Inside, the white marble floors were polished smooth as ice. The walls were hung with bright tapestries. Great fires burned in every room.

"Welcome, my dear!" The Queen of Ice Mountain greeted Lily with open arms.

Servants took Lily's cloak and removed her leather boots. They led her to a chamber with white fur rugs on the floor and a four-poster bed draped with rich red curtains.

"The Queen expects you at supper," a lady-in-waiting told Lily. "There is a warm bath waiting for you in your inner chamber."

Lily smiled. The bath was deep and smelled good. She lay up to her neck in bubbles, staring at the white, moulded ceiling.

Meanwhile, in the great central hall of the palace, the seven dwarves sat by a roaring fire telling stories about the gold mines, drinking and eating as much as even Roly could wish for.

This is the life! Lily thought, wrapping herself in a warm towel and finding new clothes laid out on her bed.

She put on pure white petticoats and

stockings and stepped into a long dress of cream lace decorated with pearls. Then she slipped her feet into red shoes of softest leather. She set a ruby tiara in her hair and looked in the gilded mirror.

"Safe at last!" she murmured, straightening her tiara and running her hand over the creamy lace gown.

Then she left her chamber and went down to supper.

4

"This is better than meat pie and potatoes, eh, Roly?" Will beamed across the supper table at his brother.

The table was piled high with roasted meats and juicy vegetables. Wine was served in silver goblets. On the balcony overlooking the great hall, a hundred violinists played.

Roly grinned and tucked in. With rosy

cheeks Walt and Hans drank their wine. Will joked with the serving girls, while Tom and Pete talked through the day's events.

"The Queen is a kind woman," Pete said. "See how she has placed Snow White beside her."

Tom agreed. "She's like a mother to her. We were right to seek her out and trust her with Snow White's happiness."

Soon the plates were cleared and the music stopped. The Queen stood up and spoke. "Now there will be a dance," she announced. "With happy tunes to cheer us on our way to bed."

Lily stood up and took a deep breath. "Here's where I wish I hadn't eaten so much!" she whispered to Hans.

"Yes, I can hardly move, let alone dance," he grinned. "Besides, I don't know the steps."

The Queen was passing by and she heard Hans's confession. "Dance with me – I will show you how!" she declared, seizing him by the hand and leading him on to the dance floor.

"Ho-ho!" Will cried, ready to laugh at his clumsy brother's expense. "Watch out for your dainty feet, Your Majesty!"

The Queen stood tall and slender in the centre of the room. Her gown was gold brocade; the long, tapered sleeves trailed down to the floor. "Put your arm around my waist," she told poor Hans.

Blushing and stumbling, he began to waltz.

Then Will asked a lady-in-waiting to dance and Walt and Jack followed him with pretty girls on their arms. Soon everyone except Lily was dancing.

Then the Prince of Ice Mountain came up to her and made a low bow. "Will you dance with me?" he asked, looking earnestly into her eyes.

"Well, you can't say no to a Prince who has just rescued you from a freezing forest filled with wolves," Lily imagined telling Amber and Pearl later. "He even fought a duel to save me from

40

Pester-Face, remember!"

So she curtsied and said yes and was soon swept around the floor, turning and whirling so that her lace skirt flew out behind her and her soft red shoes were a blur of movement. She laughed

with the Prince and danced until the music stopped.

"Snow White is happy!" Walt murmured to Jack.

The brothers had gathered by the stairs, tired after their eventful day.

"No one deserves happiness more than Snow White," Jack said with a smile.

They all nodded, and one by one the

dwarves yawned, climbed the stairs and went to bed.

"Alive?" shrieked the evil Queen Serena.

Prince Lovelace had flung himself down at the Queen's feet. Jumbled words had tumbled from his mouth. "Snow White . . . in the forest . . . riding a chestnut horse . . . with a Prince . . . seven dwarves . . . alive!"

"I left Snow White dead!" Her Most Royal Highness screamed. "Dead upon the frozen ground – poisoned!"

"Believe me, Your Most Royal Highness!"

"Idiot!" she yelled, striding across her chamber then back again. "Are you sure you saw Snow White?"

"Certain!" he whimpered. Now he

wished he'd never come back. The Queen was in a rage and he was seriously scared.

"Then you are a fool!" she cried, seizing him by his wispy beard. "You saw her and yet you let her live!"

"I could not kill her," Lovelace pleaded. "The Prince of Ice Mountain was there to defend her. I fought him with my sword!"

Queen Serena glared down at him. "You are a weak and cowardly man!" she spat. Then she called for the guards. "Take him to the dungeons. Lock him up. Let him starve!"

"Y-y-your Majesty!" Lovelace cried. "It is not my fault!"

But Queenie didn't care whose fault it was that Snow White was alive. She sneered as the soldiers took Lovelace away. "Out of my sight. I never want to see you again!"

Then she gathered her long, blood-red satin train and strode to the mirror which hung on her wall. She glared into it.

"Tell me, glass, oh tell me true!" she chanted.

"Of all the ladies in the land,

44

Who is the fairest, tell me who!"

The Queen's reflection grew blurred but the magic mirror was silent.

Queen Serena clenched her fists. "Who is the fairest?" she hissed. "Tell me who!"

And the mirror eventually replied. "Thou, Queen, art fairest in all this land."

Then the Queen gasped and clapped her hands. "Lovelace was wrong!" she cried. "He did not see Snow White in the forest. He was mistaken!"

And she would have danced for joy if the mirror had not spoken again.

"But beyond the forest, on the mountain high,

Where seven dwarves on their pillows lie,

There Snow White hides her head, and she,

Is lovelier far, O Queen, than thee!"

Then the Queen's blood ran cold and her heart twisted with jealousy. She stamped her feet, swearing that she would seek out Snow White once more. "And this will be the last time!" she raged. "However far Snow White flees, I will find her. Her friends will not stop me – for I am Queen of this land and no man will disobey me!"

5

Next morning Lily had breakfast with the Queen of Ice Mountain.

"How did you enjoy the dance?" the Queen asked between mouthfuls of bread and honey.

Scared of dribbling honey down her posh lace gown, Lily tucked a napkin under her chin. "Good," she nodded. "I didn't think I could waltz, but it turns out I can."

"And my son?" the Queen went on. "How do you like him?"

"He's a good dancer." Lily sidestepped the question but felt herself blush.

"And?"

"And – well – he's a bit . . ."

". . . Soppy?" the Queen suggested.

Whoops! Lily went bright red. "Sorry, did I make it that obvious?"

The Queen laughed merrily. "It's true! The Prince is young. He falls in love at the drop of a hat."

"He does?"

"Yes, all the time. First there was Eleanor, then Margaret. After that there was Bridget and now there is you. And you are very pretty, my dear. Who could help falling in love with you? But don't worry – he'll soon get over it."

"Wow!" Suddenly Lily felt better. She decided she liked the Queen of Ice Mountain – a lot!

The Queen polished off her bread and honey then licked her fingers. "It's your poor father I feel sorry for. Serena has broken his heart with her evil tricks."

Lily sighed as she pictured King Jakob shut up inside his room, grieving for Snow White.

"Jakob is a good man," the Queen went on. "But he didn't choose well when he took Serena as his second wife."

Lily nodded. "Nobody likes Queenie. Everyone thinks she's mean."

"And jealous, greedy and cruel." The Queen listed Serena's faults, counting

49

them off on her sticky fingers. "And wicked . . . very wicked."

"So?" Lily wondered.

The Queen got up from the table and wandered to the window overlooking the mountains. "So we must make a plan to get rid of Serena," she decided. "Leave me alone for a while, my dear. I need time to think."

"Aahchoo! . . . Aaah-aah . . ."

Nurse Gretchen slid back the bolt of Prince Lovelace's prison door and gave him his breakfast.

". . . Choo!" he sneezed.

"Eat this," she told him. "And drink this tea. It will do you good."

The Prince ate the dry bread and

slurped the tea. "Aaahchoo!"

"They say you saw Snow White in the forest," Gretchen said. Snow White's faithful old Nurse had been one of the first to hear the rumour flying around the palace – "Snow White is alive! The Queen is in a rage. Lovelace is in the dungeons!"

"What of it?" Pester-Face muttered. "It did me no good to bring the message back to Her Most Royal Highness, did it?"

"No indeed," Gretchen said slowly. "But she – Snow White – *is* alive?"

"Alive and kicking. The ungrateful girl almost choked me to death! Aah-choo!"

"And is she safe?"

"Pah! Safe with the Prince of Ice Mountain. Aahchoo!"

"The handsome Prince?" Gretchen

murmured. "Hmm."

"He has taken her home to his mother's palace," Lovelace said. "And I have washed my hands of her!"

"Very good!" Gretchen stepped out of the cell and bolted the door. Her face didn't show it but her heart was bursting for joy.

Alive and kicking! Her darling, her dove, her precious song thrush was safe with friends!

But the wicked Queen knew it. And now Gretchen hurried up the stone stairs from the dungeons to the stables.

"Saddle my horse!" she told the grooms as she put on her thick cloak and gloves. "Be quick. The sun is up and I must ride through the forest in the daylight."

"Take care," the grooms warned as they heaved her into her saddle. "You are an old woman – you should not ride alone."

"Watch me!" Gretchen retorted, riding her stout grey mare out through the wide gates. "And not so much of the 'old'!" she called back.

As the Queen of Ice Mountain thought out her plan, Lily wandered through the palace.

"'My love is like a rose . . .'"

She heard the Prince's voice from inside a room lined with books. She peered round the door and saw him, pen in hand.

"'My love is like a rose . . .'" he repeated dreamily. Then he scribbled. "'. . . Her face

53

is white as snow . . .'"

Lily pulled a face. The Prince was writing love poetry!

He scratched his head. "'My love is like a rose, Her face is white as snow . . . I follow her where ever she goes!'"

Yuck! Yeah, he was handsome with his blue eyes and fair hair, but he wrote lousy poetry!

54

I need a break! Lily thought, hurrying off along the corridor, through the hall where she'd danced with the Prince. She waved at Walt, Will and Tom who were on the balcony, sitting with their feet up and chatting with some of the palace servants.

Tom stood up and watched Lily head out of the main door. "Where are you off to?" he called.

"For a little walk," she answered.

"Don't go far," sensible Tom warned.

"I won't!" Lily waved again. She stepped out into the sunshine and took a deep breath of fresh air. Lifting her lace skirt clear of the snowy ground, she walked past the sentries at the gate, out into the woods.

Two red squirrels scampered up a tree

trunk then peered down at her from a low branch.

Pretty! Lily thought.

A mother deer and two fawns trotted daintily across the path.

But cold! Lily had forgotten to put on her cloak and boots. Her red dancing shoes sank into the snow. She shivered then turned back towards the palace.

Oh! Seriously – oh! Lily stopped in her tracks as she heard twigs snap in the frosty undergrowth. Something was stepping stealthily between the tall trees. "Rrrr-rrrahhh!" it growled.

What was it? A bear or a mountain lion? A wolf?

The creature prowled towards her, still hidden.

Whatever it was, it didn't sound friendly. Lily started to run.

"Wrrraaagh!" The big wolf sprang out of the undergrowth. Its eyes were yellow, its teeth sharp and glistening. And it had Lily in its sights.

"Help!" Lily cried out. "Somebody, help me!"

6

A horse thundered down the path towards Lily and the wolf.

"Help!" Lily screamed.

The wolf stared at Lily and licked its lips. Its yellow eyes drilled into her.

As the horse drew near, Lily darted off the path and began to run through the trees. The wolf bounded after her. She could hear it panting, almost feel its hot breath on her.

"Don't be afraid, Snow White my dove – I'll save you!" The horse and rider blundered into the shadowy wood. The grey horse jumped fallen trees; the rider seized a loose branch as the wolf got ready to pounce.

"Oh!" Lily gasped. She stumbled and fell headlong into a snowdrift.

The wolf crouched over her, its fangs bared.

"Oh no you don't!" Nurse Gretchen cried, taking a swipe at the wolf with the thick branch. She walloped it and sent it rolling down the hill. Then she charged after it on her horse.

Now Lily was up on her feet, staring at the old Nurse with her skirts and petticoats flying, wondering how she'd got here and thanking her lucky stars.

"Take that!" Gretchen yelled, bashing the wolf a second time.

The wolf yelped then flattened its ears. It growled viciously at its attacker.

"Watch out!" Lily warned. The wolf had been taken by surprise, but now it was ready to fight back.

"Think of yourself, Snow White. Run to the palace and leave me to deal with Mr Wolf!"

"I'm staying!" Lily decided. No way would she desert brave Gretchen.

"Then jump up on my horse," the Nurse muttered, raising the branch above her head like a heavy club and waiting for Lily to climb up behind her. "Good. Take that, you ugly beast!" *Whack-whack!* "That's for scaring my own little dove. And that! And that!"

"Wow!" Lily was impressed. Gretchen had landed lots more hefty thumps. The wolf lay flattened in the snow.

But only for a second. Because now he was up on his feet again, his pink tongue lolling, teeth flashing in the sunlight as he moved in.

Lily put her arms round the Nurse's stout waist and held on. The horse reared and struck out at the wolf with her hooves.

"Hold tight!" Gretchen cried.

"Wrrraagh!" Mr Wolf roared. It had the enemy on the run. The mare backed off under a tree, Gretchen and Lily shrieked with fright.

"Help! Help!" Gretchen and Lily screamed.

And seven sturdy figures ran down the path. They wielded seven sharp pickaxes and let out seven deep yells as they burst on to the scene.

"Charge!" Jack yelled, leading the attack.

And now the wolf saw a forest full of enemies in leather jerkins and woollen hats, with gleaming weapons and angry faces. Outnumbered, he crouched low on the ground and looked for a way to escape.

The seven dwarves surrounded the wolf.

"Rrrrah!" He cowered close to the ground, tail between his legs.

"Whack it! Bash it!" Gretchen cried as she recovered. "It attacked Snow White!"

Jack, Hans, Pete, Roly, Walt, Will and Tom made a tight circle around the wolf. They crouched forward, pickaxes at the ready.

Then, in a flash, the wolf made his move. He leaped straight at Will, knocking him backwards and making a gap in the circle.

Freedom! The wolf saw it and charged through the gap before Will could prevent him. On he charged without a backward glance, until all they could see was a swift grey shadow and all they could hear was an angry howl.

"Very well." Her Most Royal Highness Queen Serena looked in her mirror with a cold stare. "I will not ask who is the fairest lady in the land until I have found Snow White and dealt with her once and for all!"

All night the Queen had lain awake plotting. *I will set off in the morning and take a small band of men with me. No one will see us. We will ride to Ice Mountain with murder in mind!*

She had risen from her bed and called for cold-blooded Sir Manfred, who stood beside her now.

"Sir Manfred is my right-hand man." The Queen spoke calmly into the mirror. "He has chosen five villains to ride with us. He will pay them well."

The carved silver mirror glinted in the early morning light. It did not speak back to the beautiful, cruel Queen, who stared at its shiny surface and saw her own face reflected there.

"I *am* lovely," she told the mirror, holding her proud head high. "There is no woman as beautiful. And when we have ridden to Ice Mountain and dealt with Snow White, I will gaze into your smooth surface and you will tell me what I long to hear – that I, Serena, am the fairest of all the ladies, near and far!"

7

"Oh dear, dear!" The Queen of Ice Mountain sighed. She wagged a warning finger at Lily. "You must never – I repeat, never – walk in the woods alone!"

Still breathless from her scary adventure with Mr Wolf, Lily nodded. "I promise I won't do it again."

The Queen broke away from her large group of advisers. "You are brave men," she told the dwarves.

Jack and the others stood to attention, with broad smiles on their rosy faces.

"I will have gold medals made for you and from now on you will be called Sir Jack, Sir Tom, Sir Will . . ." She hesitated as she tried to remember names.

"Sir Hans, Sir Pete, Sir Roly and Sir Walt!" Lily chimed with a grin. "Wow – that's a great reward!

The brothers stood with their chests puffed out. They felt ten feet tall.

Next the Queen turned to Gretchen. "And you," she said kindly, "what reward shall I give you?"

"None at all!" the old Nurse declared, folding her arms across her chest. "Knowing that my darling dove is safe is the only reward I need!"

Lily braced herself for one of Gretchen's big hugs. And sure enough, the Nurse threw her arms around her, half smothering her.

"A fine gown, maybe?" the Queen inquired. "Some new shoes or a hat?"

"A hat?" Gretchen echoed. She seemed pleased at the idea. "Could it be made of green velvet and trimmed with black fur?"

"Perhaps," the Queen said with a smile.

"And could it have a wide brim with a long veil, and fine purple feathers to decorate the crown?"

"Whatever you wish."

Gretchen clasped her hands and did a

merry jig. "Then I will have just such a hat!" she cried.

"And now," the Queen of Ice Mountain said with a clap of her hands. "Everyone here knows that Her Most Royal Highness Queen Serena is a jealous woman who must not be allowed to get her wicked way!"

"Hurrah! Down with Queen Serena!" the seven brothers, Gretchen, Lily and all the ladies and gentlemen gathered in the great hall cried.

"I have spent the night thinking about the problem as I promised," the Queen continued. "And this morning I have reached a decision."

Everyone held their breaths.

"I and my son, the Prince of Ice Mountain, will lead a group of soldiers down the mountain and through the forest. Snow White – you will come too."

Lily nodded cautiously.

"So will I!" Gretchen insisted. From now on she would never let Snow White out of her sight.

"And so will we!" Faithful Walt was the first to jump forward, half a step ahead of his six brothers.

"Very well," the Queen agreed. "We will all ride to King Jakob's palace and tell him of his wife's wickedness. We will show him that his daughter is alive!"

"Good!" the dwarves and Gretchen cried. "He will listen to you, Your Majesty!"

"Hurrah!" the lords and ladies shouted again.

"Come!" the Queen said, taking Lily by

the hand and swishing out through the main door. "The Prince and soldiers have saddled the horses. Time is short. Let us go!"

Queen Serena left her palace with Sir Manfred and five sly servants. The men were dressed in black cloaks with black hats pulled down to hide their faces. The Queen wore a cloak of black fur.

They rode hard – dark shadows in the forest. Deer fled as they approached. Even the foxes and wolves stayed in their dens.

"Snow White shall not see the sun set!" Serena swore. "This time I will make sure that she dies!"

"Come along, keep up!" the Queen of Ice Mountain told her followers. She rode ahead of the large group on a white horse with a red harness. The Prince rode behind with Lily. Then came the soldiers in their smart blue uniforms, then the dwarves on foot and last of all Gretchen on her grey mare.

"Are you cold, Snow White?" the Prince fussed.

"No, my cloak is keeping me warm, thanks." Not cold, but nervous. Lily couldn't help being afraid of Queenie and her sneaky tricks. She trembled inside her cloak as her horse picked its way down the sparkling mountain.

"Tarrum-tum-tum! Tarrum-tum!"

The sound of the seven brothers singing their song cheered her up. They carried their pickaxes over their shoulders, just as if they were marching to work in the gold mines. And dear old Gretchen was plodding behind.

"It's almost midday!" the Queen said, glimpsing the sun between the trees. "Hurry. We must reach the King before the sun sets!"

Queen Serena and her followers galloped through the forest until they reached a clearing.

"Stop!" she cried, spying a small cottage. She turned to Sir Manfred. "Is this the wretched place where the seven dwarves live?"

Sir Manfred nodded. "It is, Your Most Royal Highness. This is where the brothers hid Snow White. Then they lied to me and sent me off on a wild goose chase."

"Very well," the Queen said coldly. "Let's plan how we can punish them."

Sir Manfred knew the icy glare all too well. He kept quiet as the Queen worked out her revenge.

"It is a cold day," she said quietly. "Let's make it warm for the brothers when they return."

Then she ordered Sir Manfred to dismount from his horse and make a fire in the cottage hearth. *What kind of revenge is this?* he wondered as the flames flickered in the grate.

But then Her Most Royal Highness swept in through the low door and seized a burning log. She carried it out of the cottage and glanced around. "Aha!" she said, seeing that the roof was made of straw. And she held the burning log to the thatch, smiling as sparks took hold and the roof began to flare with red and orange flames.

"Good!" Serena muttered as the fire grew bigger. "It is the home of traitors. Let it burn to the ground!"

8

The flames in the clearing rose high above the treetops. Grey smoke swirled into the blue sky.

"Where is that fire?" Pete asked, pointing to the smoke on the horizon.

The Queen of Ice Mountain reined in her horse. Her procession halted.

"In our clearing," Jack quickly decided. "Your Majesty, our cottage is on fire!"

76

So the Queen ordered her soldiers and the Prince to gallop ahead. The dwarves took a short cut through the undergrowth.

"This is so-o-o bad!" Lily muttered as she and Gretchen rode with the Queen. "The dwarves won't have anywhere to live if their cottage burns down!"

"Queen Serena is behind this, mark my words," Gretchen grumbled. "A cottage doesn't set itself on fire. Someone wicked makes it happen!"

"Perhaps," the good Queen agreed, hurrying on.

"Fetch water from the stream!" Tom cried as the dwarves reached the clearing. "There are buckets in the woodshed. Be quick, or we will lose our home!"

Queen Serena heard the brothers trample through the bushes. She ordered her servants to hide behind the trees. "Hah! They are already too late," she whispered with a savage smile.

But then the Prince of Ice Mountain and his soldiers charged into the clearing on horseback and all the men formed a human chain from the stream to the burning cottage, passing buckets of water between them. Jack stood closest to the flames, quenching them as best he could.

"More!" Will ordered, running back to

the stream with an empty bucket. "Never fear – we will win this battle!"

Hiss! Water drenched the burning roof. Steam mingled with the smoke.

Queen Serena watched from her hiding place. Her face turned sour as the fire died down. And now she saw her neighbouring Queen ride into the clearing with a stout woman who gasped and muttered, followed by a young girl wrapped in a crimson cloak.

"Snow White!" she hissed in her snake-voice. "And this time she comes with

some powerful friends!"

Sir Manfred shifted uneasily. The five servants cowered low.

"It seems I must change my plan," Serena muttered. There was an uneasy pause, then a retreat. "Back to the palace!" she ordered, scuttling away like a bat, her black cloak flying.

Meanwhile, the dwarves and soldiers were beating the flames.

"The roof is gone but the rest of the house is safe!" Pete announced, his face blackened by smoke.

Roly pushed open the front door and went inside, followed by Walt and Hans. They came out again, carrying a sooty armchair and a smouldering rug.

"Stay and save your possessions," the

Queen of Ice Mountain told the dwarves. "The rest of us will ride on and visit King Jakob as planned."

Lily's heart beat faster as they drew near the palace. *I'm riding into the dragon's den!* she thought. *If you ask me, I'd rather face the wolf than Queenie any day!*

The gates were closed as the Queen and Prince of Ice Mountain rode at the head of the procession. A sentry stepped forward with the shout of "Who goes there?"

The Prince rode up to the guard. "Her Majesty the Queen of Ice Mountain wishes to speak with King Jakob," he said in a bold voice.

"The King will see no one," the sentry replied. "He stays alone in his chamber, drowning in sorrow, for his daughter, Snow White, who is dead."

At this the Queen led Lily up to the gate. "Stand aside," she told the sentry. "Run to tell the King we have good news!"

The man looked from the Queen to Lily and recognised Snow White. His jaw dropped. "Your M-M-M-Most Royal H-H-Highness!"

Lily's heart thumped. She smiled weakly at the sentry.

"Tell the King," the Queen of Ice Mountain said again.

But as the man got ready to hurry off with the news, a tall figure swept across the courtyard. She held her head high and wore a gold crown set with rubies and a dress of crimson satin. She opened her arms wide and smiled. "Can this be true?" she asked in fake amazement. "Snow White, is it really you?"

"My dear husband, Snow White is alive!" Queenie rushed ahead into King Jakob's chamber and announced the good news.

Behind her, Lily cringed. *What's with the fake smile and the snake-hugs?* she wondered.

The Queen and the Prince of Ice Mountain looked confused. But they had no time to tell the King what they thought of his wicked wife because Jakob had seen Lily.

He stood by the window in a room lit only by candlelight. His grey head was bare. He wore a long tunic of plain black.

As he looked up, his eyelids flickered and he drew a sharp breath. "Snow White?" he whispered.

Further and further into Queenie's latest web Lily was drawn. With a fast-beating heart she stepped forward but said nothing.

And no words were spoken, no questions asked as the King embraced his lost daughter.

"We are so-o-o glad!" Queen Serena sighed, clasping her ruby-ringed hands. "We can hardly believe it. It's as if a fairy waved her magic wand and brought you back to life!"

84

Fake, fake, fake! Lily thought. Thump-thump went her heart.

Gretchen glowered at Queenie and clenched her fists.

Serena took her husband's hand. "My dear, we must have a feast to celebrate Snow White's return. Tonight! With food and wine and dancing!" She turned to the Prince of Ice Mountain. "What do you say? Shall you dance with Snow White?"

"Of course, Your Most Royal Highness," the gallant Prince replied.

And so the King smiled for the first time in many weeks and said there *would* be a feast, and everyone must prepare to be glad, for Snow White had brought light back into his life, and there would be joy and happiness for ever.

*

"I curse the day Snow White was born!" Queen Serena was in her chamber, speaking into her mirror. "She has more lives than a cat!"

The mirror glittered on the wall.

"I smile and smile until my face aches," Queenie went on. "But behind the mask I choke with rage!"

She turned and paced the room. "First the feast," she muttered, turning and pacing again. "Then the dance. Enjoy it while you can, Snow White!"

Back at the mirror, the Queen gazed at her reflection. Her dark eyes glittered and her smooth brow was furrowed into a deep frown. "The feast, the dance, and then . . . the end!"

9

Lily sat at the table but she couldn't eat. She sighed at the meat piled on her silver plate and shook her head at the spiced fruit puddings.

King Jakob declared himself too happy to join in the feast. He sat at the top of the long table, eating nothing but gazing fondly at Lily. Then he ordered more wine and called for the music to begin.

Meanwhile, Queen Serena never once

left the King's side.

"She sticks to him like glue!" Gretchen grumbled to the Queen of Ice Mountain. "She sits and smiles and hides her black heart!"

"This is not what I expected," the good Queen confessed. "What is her plan?"

"She doesn't want you to speak frankly to the King." Gretchen knew Queenie of old. "She will do all in her power to prevent it."

"But sooner or later I will get him to myself," the Queen of Ice Mountain vowed as the food was cleared and the violins began to play. "If not tonight – then tomorrow. I will go to Jakob's chamber and tell him everything!"

*

Dancing on an empty stomach and with a fearful heart wasn't Lily's idea of fun.

Not that the Prince of Ice Mountain seemed to notice as he swept her around the ballroom. One-two-three, one-two-three – he waltzed her off her feet.

"I'm tired. I'd like to sit down," she sighed after the third dance.

"No, no – I will teach you the polka!" he cried, seizing her by the waist and swinging her round.

Lily was so tired she stumbled. "Ouch!" The Prince had stepped on her foot. Now she was limping too.

"Oh, your poor foot! I'm so sorry!" He blushed bright red.

His mother, the Queen, came and took pity on Lily. "Poor child, it's been a long day and you're exhausted."

Lily nodded. She allowed the Queen to take her by the hand and lead her towards the King. They pushed in front of jealous Queenie, who gave a sly frown then slipped quietly away.

"Dear Jakob, say goodnight to your daughter, before she goes up to her room," the Queen told him. "She is falling over her own feet she's so tired."

King Jakob nodded then kissed Lily on the cheek. "I am tired too and ready for bed. Sleep well, my dear. Tomorrow, when you are rested, we will talk."

He led Lily from the ballroom and at the bottom of the stairs they parted. Lily climbed the stairs. Her head seemed to swim as she trod wearily along the corridor.

Inside her own room she sank on to the bed. The candle on the table flickered. Shadows danced across the tapestries hanging from the walls.

Almost too tired to kick off her red shoes and unlace her gown of cream lace, she yawned again. There was water in a crystal glass by her bedside so she took a sip.

Wind blew through the heavy bed curtains that closed out the cold night. They stirred again as Lily had another refreshing sip then for the first time noticed a golden bowl with three red apples.

Lily looked at the fruit. "Trust Gretchen to bring water and apples to my chamber!" she said. The Nurse thought of everything – clean white sheets perfumed with lavender, warm slippers by the bed, and the rosy red fruit.

From behind the curtains Queen Serena spied. *Eat!* she said to herself. *Pick up an apple, Snow White. Take a bite!*

"I suppose I am a little bit hungry," Lily murmured, reaching out and picking up the nearest apple.

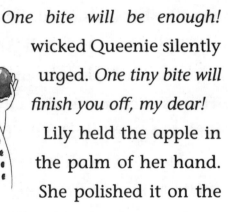

One bite will be enough! wicked Queenie silently urged. *One tiny bite will finish you off, my dear!*

Lily held the apple in the palm of her hand. She polished it on the sleeve of her dress.

Eat!

"I'm so tired!" Lily sighed, almost deciding to put the shiny apple back in the dish. But it looked juicy and sweet, and she *was* hungry . . .

One bite! One tiny bite!

Lily raised the apple to her lips. She opened her mouth and crunched into it.

That's it – one swallow! Queenie's jealous heart soared with delight.

The apple was crisp and hard to chew. Lily gulped as she tried to swallow.

But the piece of apple stuck in her throat. She choked and tried to shout for help but no sound came out.

"At last!" Serena said, stepping out triumphant from behind the curtain.

Lily couldn't breathe. She looked up and saw Queenie with her cruel smile.

Then she fell back on the bed in a deep faint.

10

"Tell me, glass, tell me true!
Of all the ladies in the land,
Who is fairest? Tell me who?"

Serena stood before her mirror. Her face was flushed, her eyes dark and glittering.

She had left Snow White's chamber and rushed down the corridor, thrusting Gretchen out of her way as the old Nurse toiled up the stairs. Now she stood gazing

94

at her reflection, waiting for the mirror to answer.

The mirror's shiny surface misted over then cleared again. When it spoke, its words were slow and low. "Thou, Queen, art fairest in the land."

The Queen's heart swelled with pride. "At last!" she murmured over and over again, with a deep, satisfied smile.

"Wake up, my dove. Snow White – wake up!" The Nurse shook Lily then patted her cheek. "I've come to unlace your gown and help you into bed. Come, my little goose, open your eyes."

But the apple had lodged in Lily's throat and she lay lifeless.

Then Gretchen saw how pale she was,

and how cold. She tried to warm her cheeks, but it was no good Then she leaned close to Lily's mouth to feel her soft breath. "Nothing!" she whispered.

In panic she ran from the chamber to fetch help.

Her desperate cries reached Jack, Hans, Roly, Pete, Tom, Will and Walt as they strode into the courtyard, weary after their long walk from the cottage.

"Snow White is dead!" Gretchen sobbed. And the whole palace heard. "She lies lifeless on her bed!"

So the dwarves raced up the stairs and they too saw Lily lying still and pale as a marble statue.

"Wake up!" Walt pleaded, while Roly covered her with blankets.

Tom and Pete ran for a doctor. Jack and Will spoke urgently into Lily's ear. "Come, my dear, wake up. Open your eyes, even just a little!"

Hans sank to his knees by the bedside, weeping silently.

It was no good. The doctor came, and the Queen of Ice Mountain with the Prince. Then King Jakob arrived and hung his head in fresh sorrow.

And all the dark night, Lily lay with the piece of apple lodged in her throat.

In the morning, the seven dwarves made a glass coffin for Snow White. They set it on a golden base and polished the glass until it shone. Then they carried it to her chamber.

Evil Queen Serena saw them with the fine casket and for the first time came to view the body of Snow White. The Queen was decked out in green satin and lace, with emeralds at her throat. A smile played at the corners of her mouth which she scarcely bothered to conceal.

She saw the King there, looking like a ghost, and Nurse Gretchen, weeping into her apron. The foolish Prince of Ice Mountain knelt at the foot of Snow White's bed, with his meddling mother.

And now Serena stood aside to let the seven dwarves approach with the casket. They set it down by the side of the bed and raised the glass lid. Then Roly and Hans lifted Lily from the bed.

"Carry her carefully!" Jack murmured.

"Gently!" Will sighed.

I am the fairest! Queenie gloated. *There is no one in the land lovelier than me!*

"She's light as a feather!" Roly said, as he and Hans carried Lily towards the casket.

Unsteadily Hans stepped backward. Clumsy as ever, he tripped on the furry slippers Gretchen had left by Lily's bed.

"Oh!" There was a loud gasp as Hans let go of Lily and Will leaped forward to help Roly.

And at that moment, as if by magic, the piece of apple dislodged from Lily's throat and she breathed again.

11

When King Jakob heard how Queen Serena had three times tried to kill Snow White, he banished her to the snowy wilderness. "From now on wolves will be her companions!" he declared.

So Queenie took her magic mirror from the wall and smashed it into a thousand pieces. She left the palace and all her fine clothes and jewels. On her lonely journey into the furthest forest, rage marked her features. Her face was bitter and as ugly as sin.

Meanwhile, the kingdom rejoiced.

"The King has got rid of Queenie!" The servants slapped each other on the back and set up three cheers. "Hurrah!"

"The Queen of Ice Mountain will sit by him at supper tonight," others reported. "She is as kind and generous as Serena was cruel and mean."

Everyone nodded and smiled, and said what a good match King Jakob and the Queen of Ice Mountain would make one day.

102

"And perhaps Snow White and the handsome Prince," they added with bright, knowing smiles.

"Good riddance to bad rubbish!" Gretchen said as she stood at a high window watching Serena disappear into the snowy forest.

"Tarrum-tum-tum!" the seven dwarves sang as they loaded straw for their cottage roof on to a cart in the courtyard.

Lily joined in – "Tarrum-tum-tum!" She helped them with the straw and gave carrots to the cart-horse.

"Goodbye, *Sir* Jack, *Sir* Tom, *Sir* Roly, *Sir* Will, *Sir* Walt, *Sir* Pete . . ." She hugged them each in turn. ". . . And *Sir* Hans!" she said as he brought the final load of straw from the stable.

The brothers got ready to march. "Tarrum-tum-tum. Tarrum . . ."

Jack drove the cart through the gates, the others followed. "Goodbye, Snow White!" they called. "Come and visit when our roof is mended!"

"I will!" Lily sighed as she watched them go. Their voices faded. She turned and went upstairs.

Nurse Gretchen had smoothed her pillow and turned down her sheets. And even though it was still daylight, Lily lay down on the bed.

"So-o-o tired!" she yawned.

A golden sun shone through the windows. Specks of dust danced in the air. Lily felt woozy, her thoughts were drifting. *Time for a nap!*

Her head sank into the pillow, the golden light grew brighter as it shone on the bed.

I'm floating! Lily thought as her eyelids flickered. *Now I'm dizzy. I'm melting into a shining white cloud – spinning, whooshing through the air!*

"Cool!" Lily smiled as she lifted the lid of Amber's dressing-up box.

Pearl and Amber rubbed their eyes. "What are you grinning at?" Amber asked Lily.

"It's OK, no need to explain!" As Lily climbed out of the box, Pearl saw her gorgeous lace dress and red dancing shoes. "You've been Snow White-ing!"

Lily nodded. "I got to dance with the handsome Prince," she told them.

"Never mind that – let me try on those shoes," Pearl pleaded. "Are they magic? Will they whoosh me away?"

"And do I get to try the lace dress?" Amber asked. "Please, Lily!"

But a call from upstairs told the girls that Amber's mum wanted to take them to the shops. "You can have ice cream if you've done the tidying up and come quickly!"

So Pearl kicked off the red shoes and Amber left the lace dress lying on the basement floor. They were all halfway up the stairs when Lily turned back.

"Ice cream if we're *quick*!" Amber reminded her.

"Yeah, let's get a move on," Pearl said. "Lily – where are you going?"

"To finish tidying up," Lily replied.

"I'll come and help you," Pearl decided. The girls rushed downstairs and threw the dressing-up clothes in the box. All except for an old-fashioned red shawl that they'd never seen before.

"Where did this come from?" Pearl wondered.

"Dunno," Lily shrugged. "But come on – we'll be late for ice cream."

"Race you there!" Pearl cried, taking the stairs two at a time.

Have you checked out...

www.dressingupdreams.net

It's the place to go for games, downloads, activities, sneak previews and lots of fun!

You'll find a special dressing-up game and lots of activities and fun things to do, as well as news on Dressing-Up Dreams and all your favourite characters.

Sign up to the newsletter at **www.dressingupdreams.net** to receive extra clothes for your Dressing-Up Dreams doll and the opportunity to enter special members only competitions.

What happens next...?
Log on to www.dressingupdreams.net for a sneak preview of my next adventure!

WIN A Dressing-Up Dreams GOODIE BAG!

CAN YOU SPOT THE TWO DIFFERENCES AND THE HIDDEN LETTER IN THESE TWO PICTURES OF LILY?

There is a spot-the-difference picture and hidden letter in the back of all four Dressing-Up Dreams books about Lily (look for the books with 6, 7 or 8 on the spine). Hidden in one of the pictures above is a secret letter. Find all four letters and put them together to make a special Dressing-Up Dreams word, then send it to us. Each month, we will put the correct entries in a draw and one lucky winner will receive a magical Dressing-Up Dreams goodie bag including an exclusive Dressing-Up Dreams keyring!

Send your magical word, your name and your address
on a postcard to: **Lily's Dressing-Up Dreams Competition**

UK Readers:
Hodder Children's Books
338 Euston Road
London NW1 3BH
marketing@hodder.co.uk

Australian Readers:
Hachette Children's Books
Level 17/207 Kent Street
Sydney NSW 2000
childrens.books@hachette.com.au

New Zealand Readers:
Hachette Livre NZ Ltd
PO Box 100 749
North Shore City 0745
childrensbooks@hachette.co.nz

Only one entry per child. Final draw: 30th August 2009
For full terms and conditions go to www.hachettechildrens.co.uk/terms

COLOURING FUN!

Carefully colour the Dressing-Up Dreams picture
on the next page and then send it in to us.

Or you can draw your very own fairytale
character. You might want to think about what
they would wear or if they have special powers.

Each month, we will put the best entries
on the website gallery and one lucky winner
will receive a magical Dressing-Up Dreams
goodie bag!

Send your drawing, your name and
your address on a postcard to:
Lily's Dressing-Up Dreams Competition

UK Readers:
Hodder Children's Books
338 Euston Road
London NW1 3BH
kidsmarketing@hodder.co.uk

Australian Readers:
Hachette Children's Books
Level 17/207 Kent Street
Sydney NSW 2000
childrens.books@hachette.com.au

New Zealand Readers:
Hachette Livre NZ Ltd
PO Box 100 749
North Shore City 0745
childrensbooks@hachette.c

For full terms and conditions go to www.hachettechildrens.co.uk/terms

Lily's Dressing-Up Dreams

The Lace Gown

COMING SOON

Pearl's Dressing-up Dreams

Lily's Dressing-Up Dreams

The Lace Gown

JENNY OLDFIELD

Hodder
Children's
Books

A division of Hachette Children's Books

Hodder Children's Books
A division of Hachette Children's Books
338 Euston Rd, London NW1 3BH
An Hachette Livre UK company